A blessing especially for

______________________________

# *A Blessing for*
# AUTUMN'S CHILD

*Words by* PETER HINCKLEY

BUSHEL & PECK BOOKS

Dearest child of autumn,
may the bounty of your
season always live within you.

May each day be as rich as the farmer's harvest . . .

. . . as warm as
baking pumpkin . . .

. . . and as sweet as the
first of autumn's apples.

May the autumn wind be
ever at your back . . .

... the sun warm
upon your face ...

. . . and the leaves soft
beneath your feet.

May you soar like the geese on life's sunny days . . .

... run like
the deer in
its carbuncle
forests ...

. . . bend like the willow
when its winds blow . . .

. . . and always have the
strength of the ancient
oak, who knows that no
storm lasts forever.

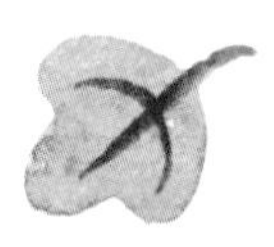

May you always be filled with the loving glow that is your season . . .

. . . of crackling fires . . .

. . . of family . . .

. . . of stars that shine in a
crisp, smoky night.

May all of autumn
remind you what
a joy you are to the world!

The birds that
sing for you . . .

. . . the pumpkins that grin for you . . .

. . . the fields that spin gold for you . . .

. . . and the leaves that
dance with delight at the
very mention of your name.

May all your days burst with the joy and color that are your birthright to have:

The red of the apple, to remind you to be give generously.

The orange of the
maple, to remind
you to smile.

The yellow of the squash, to
remind you to give thanks.

The green of the fir, to
remind you to soar.

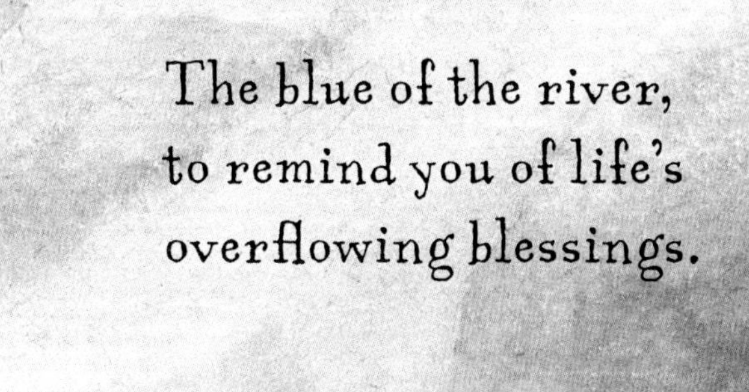

The blue of the river,
to remind you of life's
overflowing blessings.

The violet of the
mountains, to remind
you that you are destined
for great heights.

For you, child of autumn, are all that is good, all that is bright, all that is beautiful in this blessed time of year.

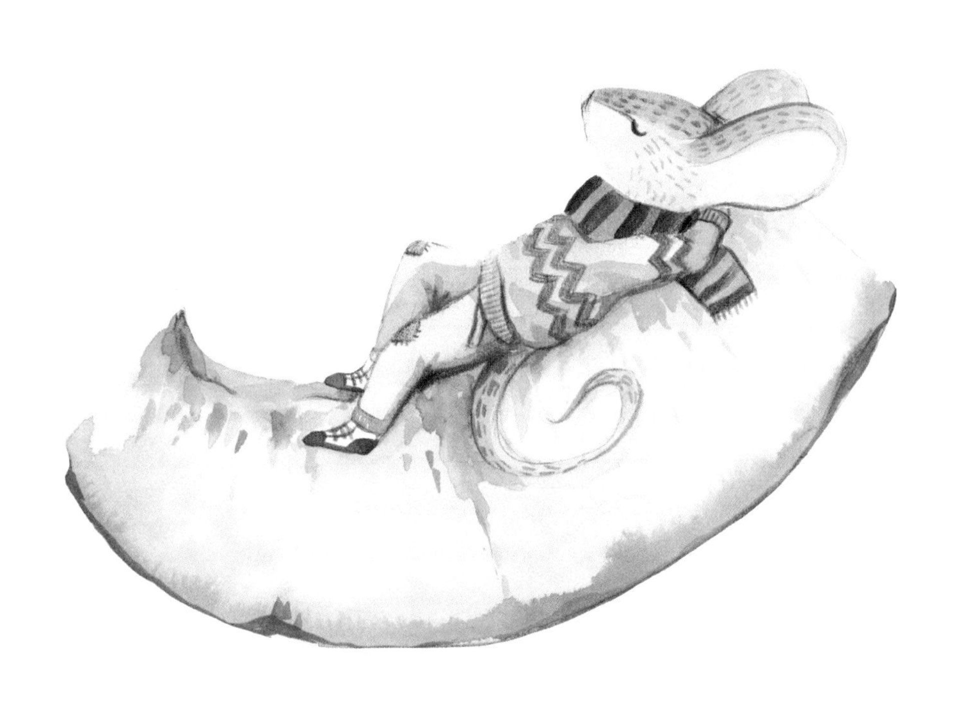

And that makes you
special, indeed.

## ABOUT BUSHEL & PECK BOOKS

Bushel & Peck Books is a children's publishing house with a special mission. Through our Book-for-Book Promise™, we donate one book to kids in need for every book we sell. Our beautiful books are given to kids through schools, libraries, local neighborhoods, shelters, nonprofits, and also to many selfless organizations that are working hard to make a difference. So thank you for purchasing this book! Because of you, another book will make its way into the hands of a child who needs it most.

If you liked this book, please leave a review online at your favorite retailer. Honest reviews spread the word about Bushel & Peck—and help us make better books, too!

## NOMINATE A SCHOOL OR ORGANIZATION TO RECEIVE FREE BOOKS

Do you know a school, library, or organization that could use some free books for their kids? We'd love to help! Please fill out the nomination form on our website (see below), and we'll do everything we can to make something happen.

www.bushelandpeckbooks.com/pages/nominate-a-school-or-organization

Published by Bushel & Peck Books, a family-run publishing house in Fresno, California, that believes in uplifting children with the highest standards of art, music, literature, and ideas. Find beautiful books for gifted young minds at www.bushelandpeckbooks.com.

Type set in Aunt Mildred and IM Fell English Pro

Artwork licensed from Shutterstock.com

Bushel & Peck Books is dedicated to fighting illiteracy all over the world. For every book we sell, we donate one to a child in need—book for book. To nominate a school or organization to receive free books, please visit www.bushelandpeckbooks.com.

ISBN: 9781638190028

First Edition

Printed in the United States

10 9 8 7 6 5 4 3 2 1